**Based on the Screenplay "Scooby-Doo and the Cyber Chase"
by Mark Turosz**

Adapted by Jenny Markas

SCHOLASTIC INC.
New York   Toronto   London   Auckland   Sydney
Mexico City   New Delhi   Hong Kong   Buenos Aires

ISBN 0-439-31391-0

Special thanks to Duendes del Sur for interior illustrations
Designed by Maria Stasavage

12 11 10 9 8 7 6 5 4 3 2 1   1 2 3 4 5 6/0
Printed in the U.S.A.
First Scholastic printing, October 2001

CHAPTER ONE

"Hey, you kids! Where do you think you're going?" The big, red-faced security guard called out to Scooby and the gang. The name-tag on his uniform said "Wilbur T. Wembley."

Fred, Velma, Daphne, Shaggy, and Scooby-Doo had just arrived on the university campus in the Mystery Machine.

"We're on our way to see our friend Eric Staufer," Velma explained. "He's a student here, and he's working with Dr. Kaufman on some very important projects."

"And on a very cool computer game," Shaggy added. "Like, starring us!"

But Officer Wembley didn't seem impressed. "I don't like a whole bunch of hooligans running around my university."

"*Your* university?" Daphne asked, surprised.

Scooby snuck around behind Officer Wembley, stole his hat, put it on, and started mimicking the sourpuss security guard. The rest of the gang could hardly keep from laughing.

"That's right," Officer Wembley said. "I've worked here for over twenty years and I know every square inch of this campus." He puffed out his chest. Behind him, Scooby puffed out *his* chest. Officer Wembley whirled around and caught Scooby in the act.

"Roops!" Scooby said as Officer Wembley snatched his hat back.

The gang scurried off to Dr. Kaufman's lab before Officer Wembley could yell at them again.

They found Eric there, working hard.

"Wow, Eric, this is one groovy setup!" Daphne said admiringly, looking around at all the scientific equipment.

"Thanks! Guys, meet my lab partner and the world's biggest baseball fan, Bill McLemore," Eric said, introducing a red-haired student in a baseball cap, lab coat, and jeans.

"Nice to meet you," said Fred. He and Bill shook hands and talked a little about baseball.

After the introductions, Shaggy turned to Eric. "So, like, can we play that computer game?"

"Nobody plays that game until we get to the bottom of what happened last night." The gang turned to see Dr. Kaufman, who was wearing a long white lab coat. His hair was wild, and his glasses were smudged.

"This is the mystery gang I based my game on," Eric told Dr. Kaufman. He introduced everyone.

"Looks like you got here just in time to help us solve a high-tech mystery," said Dr. Kaufman.

"A mystery?" asked Velma.

"What happened?" asked Fred.

"Something went wrong with our hyper-energy laser last night." Eric led the gang over to a huge, complicated piece of equipment. "We use this to beam objects into cyberspace." He showed them the "Scooby-Doo and the Cyber Chase" game on his computer. "The way this game works," he explained, "is that you have to outwit all kinds of monsters and villains and find a box of Scooby Snacks on each level. As soon as you find them, you'll go to the next level." He smiled. "And this is how I got the Scooby Snacks in there." He held up a box of Scooby Snacks, then put them on a table and focused the laser on them. In moments, the box disappeared from the table — and reappeared on the computer screen!

"That's amazing!" said Velma.

"It is," said Dr. Kaufman. "Eric and Bill are sure to win the quarter-million-dollar grand prize at the International Science Fair."

"But last night, the laser beamed something from cyberspace into the real world," Eric told them. "A virus."

"R-r-rirus?" asked Scooby, looking scared.

"A freaky-looking Phantom Virus," Eric said. "And it nearly destroyed the lab!"

"Where exactly did it come from?" Daphne asked.

"From Eric's computer game," Bill said, pointing to the computer screen. "I knew we should have used my baseball game instead."

"It — it just showed up," Eric said apologetically.

"But I thought viruses had to be created," Velma said.

"Then whoever created it will be in serious trouble," said Professor Kaufman.

"We'll *all* be in trouble if we don't find that virus!" Eric said.

"How can we help?" asked Velma.

"If you can lure the Phantom Virus here, I can beam it back into the game," Eric said.

"Like, we're supposed to be Phantom Virus bait?" Shaggy asked. "No way!"

"Ro ray," agreed Scooby.

But both of them agreed to help after Eric beamed the Scooby Snacks out of the computer game and handed them over to his food-loving friends.

"You can stop the Phantom Virus with these super-magnets," Professor Kaufman told the gang, giving them each a long, flat piece of black metal.

When Scooby held up his magnet, all the tacks flew off a nearby bulletin board and landed on it. "Ruh-roh," he said.

"Those are strong magnets," said Daphne.

"Let's put them to the test," said Fred. "Let's split up and find that Phantom Virus."

CHAPTER TWO

The gang left Dr. Kaufman's lab to search the rest of the science building. They had their magnets in hand. Shaggy and Scooby headed off to the right while Daphne, Fred, and Velma headed to the left.

"Hey, you guys!" said Fred. "I didn't say *how* we were going to split up!"

"Do we ever do it any other way?" Shaggy asked, shrugging his shoulders. "Let's go, Scooby."

"Reah, ret's ro."

They walked off, leaving the other three staring after them. Then Daphne asked, "Where should we look?"

"Hmm," said Velma. "Viruses thrive in cold, damp places."

A few minutes later, the three kids were searching the basement, which was cold, damp, and very, very dusty. It was filled with outdated furniture, books, and computers from the science department, and a lot of other junk.

Velma placed her magnet on the ground and picked up a book. She blew the dust off it — straight into the face of the Phantom Virus!

"AAAAACHOOOO!" he sneezed.

"Jinkies!" cried Velma.

The Phantom Virus threw back his head and cackled wildly. Fred, Velma, and Daphne stared at it in disbelief. The monster looked like a giant bolt of electricity. He was always on the move, always shooting off sparks as he darted around. He had an evil face with a nasty grin, and long, scary fingers.

The Virus reached for Velma. But he accidentally stepped on the magnet on the floor. He screamed in pain as he started to break up electronically. The Virus yanked his foot off the magnet and ran out of the room yelling, "You'll pay for this!"

Fred, Velma, and Daphne looked at one another, then chased after the Virus.

After searching the basement, the gang saw something ahead of them.

"This way!" cried Fred. "I see a glow."

The gang tiptoed as close as they could, holding their magnets ready. They tiptoed around a corner and —

"Officer Wembley!" cried Velma.

Sure enough, it was the security guard, shining his flashlight. "This is a restricted area," he said. "You're all coming with me, back to Dr. Kaufman's lab."

"But —" Fred began.

"No buts," said Officer Wembley firmly. He led them back to the lab.

Meanwhile, Scooby and Shaggy were chowing down in the cafeteria. Each of them had a tray piled high with hot dogs, hamburgers, and fries. They ate until every scrap of food had disappeared, and then they had giant ice cream sundaes for dessert. "I know we cleaned out the whole cafeteria," Shaggy said, patting his stomach, "but I'm still hungry."

Scooby nodded in agreement. Then his eyes grew round as he stared behind Shaggy. "Ruh-roh!" he said.

Shaggy turned to see the Phantom Virus. "Yikes!" he cried. He jumped up and started running, with Scooby right behind him and the Phantom Virus, laughing that crazy laugh, right behind Scooby.

The Virus chased Shaggy and Scooby all over the building. They started in the psychology lab, where they pretended to give him a test; to the biology lab, where they let all the monkeys and rabbits out of their cages. Then they raced to the chemistry lab, where they caused a huge explosion; to the robotics lab, where Shaggy and Scooby almost caught the Virus using giant robot arms. Finally, they managed to lose the Virus in the library and dashed back to the lab to find the rest of the gang.

Fred, Velma, and Daphne were back in the lab under the watchful eye of Officer Wembley. They were waiting for Dr. Kaufman.

"I'm worried about Shaggy and Scooby," said Daphne.

Just then, the door burst open and Shaggy and Scooby ran in. "Help!" cried Shaggy.

"Relp!" yelped Scooby. The Phantom Virus was right behind them.

The Virus chased Shaggy and Scooby all over the lab, while Fred, Velma, and Daphne chased the Virus. Officer Wembley tried to stop them, but he was powerless to stop the chaos.

The gang went around and around, running in every direction. Suddenly, there was a huge crash as they all ran into one another and landed in a huge heap on the lab floor.

Just then, the hyper-energy laser came to life. It made a loud humming sound, and then it blasted a huge green beam of light — right onto the gang! As the beam focused on the gang, all five of them began to disappear. A moment later, there was nothing to see but the bare lab floor.

CHAPTER THREE

"Jinkies!" Velma gasped, as the gang slowly reappeared. Now they were all wearing space suits with big puffy arms and legs, huge helmets over their heads, and oxygen packs on their backs. And they weren't in the lab anymore. The landscape around them was gray and full of craters and big, jagged rocks.

They were on the moon.

Fred looked around. "We've been beamed inside Eric's Scooby game!" he guessed.

Shaggy started to bound along, testing how it felt to run on the moon. "Check this out!" he cried, taking gigantic strides. "I'm, like, a superhero!" He lifted a giant rock over his head. "Look! It's Super Shaggy!"

"Be careful, Shaggy," warned Velma.

"Velma's right," Fred said. "There's a lot less gravity on the moon."

Daphne looked around. "Wow. The moon sure is cold and lonely."

"I don't think we're going to be alone long," Fred said. "Remember what Eric said about his computer game? There are monsters and creatures on every level."

"Zoinks! There's our first one now!" yelled Shaggy, pointing. The Phantom Virus was standing on a rock near the gang.

"He must have gotten beamed into the game, too!" Velma said. "Back in the lab we were hunting for him, but now the tables are turned."

"Yeah," agreed Shaggy. "Now we're on his turf."

The Virus burst into a loud cackle.

The gang took off running, looking over their shoulders. The Phantom Virus disappeared for a few moments, then showed up again, this time with two evil-looking astronauts dressed in dark space-suits. Their faces were completely hidden by their black helmets. "Let's play ball!" cried the Phantom Virus, sending the astronauts toward the gang.

"Run for it!" Shaggy cried.

The gang leaped and bounded across the lunar landscape, hoping that their oxygen would last long enough to outrun the evil astronauts. "I bet if we play this game long enough, we can find out who created the Phantom Virus," Velma gasped, when they stopped to catch their breath.

"That's right!" said Fred. "I bet there are clues on each level."

"All I care about right now is getting off this level," Daphne said.

"We need to find the box of Scooby Snacks," Velma remembered.

"And there it is!" Shaggy cried, pointing toward the spot where American astronauts once landed on the moon. Right under the American flag was a box of Scooby Snacks.

"Wow," said Daphne. "That was easy."

"This is only the first level," Shaggy reminded her.

Suddenly, the Phantom Virus and the evil astronauts showed up again.

"What do we do?" cried Daphne.

"Rover!" Scooby said. "Rover!"

The gang looked around and saw a lunar rover, a vehicle made for riding on the moon. It was decorated just like the Mystery Machine!

"Hop in!" yelled Fred. Everybody jumped in and Fred drove off, going as fast as he could. The Phantom Virus and the astronauts jumped into their own rover and chased after them, throwing electrical bolts.

Suddenly, the gang's rover stopped. "I think we're out of gas!" groaned Fred. "And we're so close!"

The lunar landing site was only a few leaps away. Scooby jumped out of the rover and tried to start running. It took him a while to get enough traction to get going, but once he did he covered the ground in no time. The astronauts jumped out of their rover and chased him. Just as he got close to the flag, Scooby turned in midair and ducked. The evil astronauts missed Scooby and banged their heads together. They fell to the ground, dazed.

"Go, Scooby!" shouted Fred.

"Grab those Snacks!" yelled Shaggy.

"You're all clear, Scooby!" Daphne called.

Scooby took one more huge leap and landed right under the flag. He picked up the box in his two front paws. And as the gang started cheering, they all began to disappear.

CHAPTER FOUR

"Where are we now?" Daphne asked, when the gang reappeared. They were standing in the hot sun in the middle of a huge, dusty arena surrounded by bleachers made out of stone. The whole place looked like an ancient version of a football stadium.

"If I'm not mistaken," Velma said, looking around, "we're inside the Colosseum."

"Rolosseum?" Scooby looked puzzled.

"That's right, Scooby," Fred said. "In ancient Rome, people gathered in the Colosseum to watch events."

"Like, sports and music?" Shaggy asked.

"Well, yes," Velma said. "But the Colosseum is

most famous as the place where Roman emperors fed people to the lions."

"R-rions?" Scooby started shaking.

Velma gave him a reassuring pat. "Did anyone come up with a clue on the Phantom Virus?"

Fred crouched down on the dirt floor. "I think I found one right here in front of us." He pointed to some large lines drawn in the dust. They enclosed a diamond-shaped area of the Colosseum floor.

Velma bent to examine the lines. "I don't re-member hearing anything about lines in the Colos-seum," she said.

"Rirus! Rirus!" Scooby started shouting.

Sure enough, the Phantom Virus had arrived. He was carrying a shield and holding a huge sword. He stood near a huge door held shut by thick chains. "Let me introduce you to the home team!" he cack-led as he swung his sword to cut the chains. Out came three Roman gladiators, carrying spears, swords, and shields of their own.

Scooby started shaking again when he saw that the gladiators were skeletons!

"Whoa," said Shaggy. "Those guys look like they've got a bone to pick, huh, Scoob?"

Scooby was too terrified to answer.

The Virus used his sword to break the chains on another door. "And now for the home team's mascot," he declared. A huge, ferocious lion emerged, carrying a box of Scooby Snacks in its mouth. The lion dropped the box of Scooby Snacks. Then it let out a horrible roar.

At that, Scooby took off running. The rest of the gang wasn't far behind.

The bony gladiators let out a scream and started to give chase. One of the gladiators threw a net and Shaggy got tangled in it. He fell to the ground.

The gang tried to pull the net off, but couldn't.

"What are we going to do?" asked Daphne.

Just then, Scooby skidded to a halt. "Rhariot!" he cried. Sure enough, there was a chariot, decorated just like the Mystery Machine!

"But there are no horses to pull it!" Daphne said.

Fred looked over at Shaggy and Scooby.

Moments later, Scooby was in the harness and

Shaggy was in the chariot, driving. They tore around the Colosseum with the skeleton gladiators chasing after them. Scooby was whimpering, and Shaggy was so scared he had his eyes closed.

Meanwhile, Fred, Daphne, and Velma were being stalked by the lion. "Hand me your jacket, Daphne," Fred said. "I know it's not red, but the lion won't mind."

Reluctantly, Daphne handed over her jacket. Fred started playing matador, teasing the lion as if it were a bull. Daphne and Velma stood by, holding open the doors to the lion's cage as Fred teased it in that direction. Finally, the lion took one last charge at Fred. Fred stepped aside, the lion went straight into the cage, and Daphne and Velma slammed the door shut!

But there was no time to celebrate. The skeleton gladiators had just broken one of the wheels off Scooby and Shaggy's chariot. As Shaggy tumbled onto the ground, the net unraveled around him. He was free! "Hang in there, guys!" shouted Fred. "If you can distract the gladiators, I can grab the Scooby Snacks!"

The gladiators threw spears at Scooby and Shaggy. They almost hit them! Shaggy and Scooby grabbed the gladiators' spears and pole-vaulted up into the stone bleachers, right into the emperor's box. They ducked down for a second, then stood up, dressed in fancy Roman clothes. "Friends, Romans, and spooky gladiators!" announced Shaggy. "All hail Emperor Scooby!"

The skeleton gladiators stopped in their tracks and bowed down to show their respect. Scooby and Shaggy smiled and walked past the bowing warriors. But unfortunately, Shaggy accidentally stepped on Scooby's tunic and pulled it off. Seeing this, the skeleton gladiators raised their swords to strike the two friends.

Just then, Fred ran out onto the Colosseum floor, grabbed the Scooby Snacks, and began to disappear. Then Velma and Daphne began disappearing. And up in the emperor's box, Shaggy and Scooby started to fade away, too.

CHAPTER FIVE

"Hmmm, looks like we've been sent to the jungle," said Fred, when the gang reappeared. Sure enough, they were in the middle of a lush, tropical forest. Daphne pulled a gorgeous flower off a nearby plant and stuck it in her hair.

Just then, there was a terrible shrieking sound. The gang looked up to see a huge pterodactyl about to dive-bomb them!

"It's a *prehistoric* jungle!" yelled Velma, as everybody ducked.

"Check out the brontosaurus," Fred said, pointing toward a gigantic creature wading in a shallow lake nearby.

"Zoinks!" yelled Shaggy, pointing in the other direction.

It was the Phantom Virus, riding on a Tyrannosaurus rex. The enormous dinosaur crashed through the trees, coming toward the gang. "How's this for a big hitter?" the Virus called, laughing wildly.

The gang dove into the forest and ran for their lives. They finally managed to escape into a cave, where Scooby made a fire by rubbing two sticks together.

Velma was upset. "We just hiked through miles of jungle without finding a single clue!"

"The Phantom Virus keeps chasing us," Fred said. "There must be a reason for that."

"Hmm," said Velma. "Maybe there's a clue in what he's saying."

Meanwhile, Shaggy and Scooby were making cave drawings. Shaggy drew a charcoal drawing of an ice cream cone. He turned to Scooby to show him his work. But he was shocked to see Scooby had illed the wall with hundreds of pictures of food.

"Nice work," said Velma. "Which of you did

that one?" She pointed to another drawing, of a smoking volcano.

"Not me," Shaggy said.

"Rot re," Scooby echoed.

"I think it may be another clue," said Velma, taking a closer look. "But I'm starting to see a pattern," she continued. "Next we have to find the Scooby Snacks. And we're also going to need more wood for the fire."

Everybody looked at Shaggy and Scooby.

"It's your turn, guys," Fred said.

Shaggy and Scooby headed out into the jungle, but it wasn't long before Scooby smelled something. "Roke!" he said.

"Smoke?" Shaggy asked. He looked up to see the tops of the palm trees on fire. "Zoinks!" he said. "Where did that come from?"

"Rolcano!" Scooby said, pointing. Sure enough, a nearby volcano was erupting, shooting out flames that were setting the trees on fire. Shaggy and Scooby ran as fast as they could back to the cave to get the others.

"A volcano?" Velma asked. She looked out of the cave. "I bet that's where the Scooby Snacks are, since it's the only landmark around."

The gang jumped onto a herd of passing woolly mammoths and took a bumpy ride to the volcano. When they got there, they leaped off. "Look up there!" Daphne said.

High above them was a pterodactyl nest with a baby pterodactyl inside it.

The volcano began to rumble. "Oh, no!" cried Daphne.

"And we've got company," said Fred, pointing toward the Phantom Virus, who was riding toward them on the T-rex. He was holding a big spear. "Let's get out of here!"

The gang started climbing up the rocky cliff. Soon they were high above the Phantom Virus. "Na-na-na-na-na-na!" called Shaggy, sticking out his tongue. The Phantom Virus shook his fist and hurled his spear.

Just then, the volcano erupted, and lava began flowing down the mountain. The baby pterodactyl gave out a cry. The gang then noticed that one of his wings was pinned down by a boulder. The baby was trapped! And hot lava was flowing down toward him.

"Somebody do something!" Shaggy cried.

Scooby bravely climbed up the mountain to the baby's rescue.

Soon he had reached the pterodactyl nest and climbed inside. Scooby struggled with the boulder, and finally pushed it off the baby's wing. A box of Scooby Snacks was revealed!

The hot lava poured into the nest just as the baby lifted Scooby and flew up. Scooby managed to grab the Snacks just in time. "Scooby-Dooby-Doo!" cried Scooby.

"Man," Shaggy said, as the gang watched Scooby disappear. "If this is only the third level, we're in trouble!" Then the gang disappeared.

CHAPTER SIX

Shaggy was right. As the gang went through each level, it got harder and harder to find and grab the Scooby Snacks.

After the prehistoric jungle, they landed in an underwater world. Wearing scuba gear, they swam as fast as they could to get past the great white shark that was chasing them away from the Scooby Snacks.

Next, they arrived in what looked like a dense forest. Then they saw a giant ant, and realized that the forest was blades of grass! The gang had been shrunk. It wasn't easy to get past the ant and grab the Scooby Snacks.

After that, they had to battle an ancient Samurai warrior in a Japanese rock garden. Daphne's baton-twirling skills came in handy as she used a rake to fight him off.

The next level was medieval England, where Shaggy and Scooby had to save a beautiful maiden by fighting a dragon. Shaggy, dressed in armor, used Scooby as his horse. They managed to beat the dragon by throwing a big bucket of water into its face so it couldn't breathe fire at them.

After that, the gang was zapped into ancient Egypt, where a mummy chased them through a pyramid. The Phantom Virus showed up, riding a camel and carrying a large curved sword. They barely escaped.

Brrr . . . then the gang landed in the Arctic. They were chased by the Phantom Virus, riding the biggest polar bear they'd ever seen. The kids made it to the North Pole. Scooby wriggled up the pole and grabbed the box of Scooby Snacks while the rest of the gang fought off the Phantom Virus with snowballs.

"Phew!" said Daphne, as the gang finally reappeared on a modern city street. "We're home at last."

"I don't think so," said Fred. He pointed toward the sky. "Ever seen a sky with a grid before?" Fred asked.

"Or buildings shaped like those?" Velma asked, pointing out the oddly-shaped towers that surrounded them.

"I see cities like this all the time," Shaggy said. "They're in — zoinks! — every single video game I play."

"That's right," Fred said. "We're still in the game. But the good news is that, by my count, we're finally on the last level."

Shaggy gulped. "That means it's the hardest level."

"And we still haven't found out who created the Phantom Virus," Daphne pointed out.

"I've got a pretty good idea," Velma said. "I just need a little more proof. Let's just say I think we're in the home stretch."

"But what do we do next?" Daphne asked. "This city is so big."

"Maybe that lady over there can help us," said Fred, pointing to a woman standing nearby, wearing a heavy coat and scarf over her head. He tapped the woman on the shoulder. "Excuse me, ma'am," he said, "we're new to this city, and . . ."

The woman turned around and started laughing a wild laugh.

"Jinkies!" cried Velma. "It's the Phantom Virus!"

The Virus threw off his scarf. "Welcome to the final level!" he cackled. "You're in the major leagues now!"

"Yikes!" yelled Shaggy. "Let's get out of here!" The gang took off down the street, with the Phantom Virus chasing them.

They ran until they were all out of breath. "Let's hide in this malt shop," suggested Fred. He pushed the door open and the gang burst in. A bunch of people and a dog sat at the counter, with their backs toward the door.

"Help!" cried Daphne. "We're being chased by the Phantom Virus!"

Scooby, Shaggy, Fred, Velma, and Daphne are visiting their friend Eric, a computer programmer. Eric and his partner, Bill, have invented an amazing laser that can beam real-life things into a cool new video game — based on the Scooby gang!

Ruh-roh! A mysterious Phantom Virus has escaped from the game, and it's not very happy about being in the real world.

Just when the gang thinks they're safe from the Virus, someone beams them inside the game!

Now the gang's at the first level of the game — on the moon! They've got to play all ten levels and win to get back to reality. And if that weren't bad enough, the Phantom Virus is following them!

From level to level, Scooby, Shaggy, Fred, Velma, and Daphne must fight like gladiators...

...and escape from dinosaurs till they can find the magical box of Scooby Snacks that will transport them to the next part of the game.

Finally, the gang is back home in the real world...
or are they? It looks real, but it's actually level 10
of the video game — the hardest level of them all.

Inside the malt shop, the gang gets a
big surprise — it's their cyber-selves,
the characters from the video game!

Zoinks! Scooby and his friends finally escape the villains...only to run into the Phantom Virus inside a video arcade!

Heroic Cyber-Scooby distracts the Phantom Virus so the real Scooby can grab the Snacks and transport the gang back home.

Back in the real world, Fred, Velma, and Daphne unmask the real culprit behind the Phantom Virus — Bill, Eric's partner. Bill was so jealous of all the attention Eric got for his Scooby game, he tried to sabotage it.

Safe and sound back at home, the real Scooby gang bids their virtual buddies good-bye!

The people and the dog turned around, and the gang got a big surprise. Each one of them was a nearly perfect duplicate of a member of the gang!

"Wow," said Shaggy. "You're, like, the cyber-gang."

CHAPTER SEVEN

The gang and the cyber-gang stared at each other. Shaggy was standing right in front of Cyber-Shaggy. Fred faced Cyber-Fred. Velma and Cyber-Velma blinked at each other from behind their glasses. Daphne and Cyber-Daphne were checking out each other's outfits. And Scooby and Cyber-Scooby were just about nose-to-nose.

The cyber-gang were all wearing what they used to wear, years ago. Shaggy reached out to touch Cyber-Shaggy's chin, where there was an even scragglier goatee than his own! Cyber-Shaggy touched Shaggy's chin at the same time. "Like, wow!" Shaggy said again. "You're me."

"And, like, you're me!" Cyber-Shaggy said.

"Zoinks!" they both said at once.

Velma stared at Cyber-Velma. She wore orange knee-high stockings and a pleated skirt. "You're the characters in Eric's video game!" she said.

Cyber-Velma nodded. "And you're the *real* Scooby gang," she said.

"Jinkies!" they both said at once.

Daphne looked at Cyber-Daphne's dress. "Did I really wear that years ago?" she asked doubtfully.

Cyber-Daphne checked out Daphne's dress. "That jacket, with that skirt?" She put a finger on her chin.

"Hmmm . . ." they both said at once.

Meanwhile, Fred was looking at Cyber-Fred. "Nice ascot," he said, nodding at Cyber-Fred's orange ascot.

Cyber-Fred adjusted his ascot. "It works for me," he replied.

"Hey, over here!" called Cyber-Shaggy. He and Shaggy were already seated at a table, with a huge plate of french fries between them.

Scooby and Cyber-Scooby looked at each other. Scooby whispered into Cyber-Scooby's ear. They both giggled. A few seconds later, Scooby popped up on one side of the table, making a funny face. While Shaggy and Cyber-Shaggy were distracted, Cyber-Scooby stole the plate of fries.

Velma shook her head. "We don't have time to play around," she said. "We need to get out of here!"

"You guys are way too stressed," said Cyber-Daphne.

"You mean you guys aren't afraid of the Phantom Virus?" asked Daphne.

"Never heard of him," said Cyber-Fred, taking a sip of his milkshake.

Fred nodded. "The Phantom Virus isn't really part of this game. He has no reason to be looking for the cyber-gang."

"So, like, you guys never even saw the Phantom Virus?" Shaggy asked. "You're lucky. He's big and mean and has a really nasty laugh. It sounds like . . ."

Just then, there was a horrible, cackling laugh from outside the malt shop.

"Zoinks!" Shaggy gulped. "Just like that!"

"Come out and play!" called the Phantom Virus.

Scooby and Cyber-Scooby put their chins to the floor, covered their eyes with their paws, and started to whimper.

"It's him!" said Velma.

Sure enough, the Phantom Virus was standing right outside the malt shop.

"Let's go!" said Cyber-Fred. "The Mystery Machine is right out back!"

"I'll drive," Fred and Cyber-Fred said at the same time. Then they stopped and looked at each other.

A few seconds later, everybody was piled into the Mystery Machine as Cyber-Fred raced through the streets of the city.

"Do you know where the Scooby Snacks are?" Velma asked the cyber-gang.

"We never even looked," said Cyber-Fred. "We like things the way they are. This is a good place to live, and we don't want to get mixed up with monsters."

"But we have to find the Scooby Snacks and also

figure out who created the Phantom Virus," said Daphne.

"We have to get back to the real world and expose the culprit," agreed Velma.

"Will you guys help us?" asked Fred.

"Sure we will," said Cyber-Fred.

"Great!" said Velma. "Now, where do we look?"

"Let's think about Eric, since he designed the game," suggested Fred. "What does Eric like to do?"

"Romputers!" yelled Scooby.

"That's right," said Daphne.

"Eric loves computer games," said Velma thoughtfully.

"Where's the biggest arcade in the city?" asked Fred. "I bet we'll find the Scooby Snacks there."

"It's down by the boardwalk," said Cyber-Fred, making a quick turn in that direction.

CHAPTER EIGHT

The boardwalk was a beautiful place. When the gang and the cyber-gang piled out of the Mystery Machine, they saw the ocean along one side and a huge amusement park, with a Ferris wheel and a roller coaster, along the other. The outdoor video arcade was way down at the other end of the boardwalk.

As they were deciding where to go, they all heard a metallic dinging noise. *Clink!* They heard it again. *Clink! Clink!*

"Rase-rall!" chorused Scooby and Cyber-Scooby.

"The Scoobies are right!" said Fred. "There's a batting cage over there." Sure enough, there was somebody hitting baseballs thrown by an automatic pitcher. The batted balls went into a net. "Wow, he's really clobbering the ball!" Fred added.

This time, the batter hit the ball so hard it caught on fire. It burned right through the netting. The batter turned around and laughed a wild laugh. It was the Phantom Virus.

"Zoinks!" shouted Shaggy as the Virus began hitting ball after fiery ball right at the gang.

Velma ducked. "I think I finally have enough clues!" she said. "I know who created the Phantom Virus!"

"Save it!" said Fred. "We've got to make it to the video arcade before he does, so we can get back to the real world!"

Both gangs took off running. They were moving as fast as they could when, suddenly, a hunchbacked creature stepped out from behind a pole.

"Jeepers!" said Daphne. "It's the Creeper!"

"The what?" asked Cyber-Velma.

"The Creeper, one of the villains from our past," Fred explained.

"And he's got a friend," said Shaggy, as both gangs turned to see Jaguaro, the half ape, half saber-toothed tiger.

The gangs backed up — right into the ferocious, scaly Gator Ghoul and the gooey, dripping Tar Monster.

"Let's head for the beach!" yelled Cyber-Fred.

"Ro ray!" said Scooby. He and Cyber-Scooby pointed to the ocean, where Old Iron Face, wearing a pirate's hat and an iron mask, was riding into shore astride two mechanical sharks.

"It's like every villain we've ever faced has come back to do battle with us!" cried Velma.

"Maybe we shouldn't have told Eric so much about our mysteries," Daphne said.

"How right you are!" said a voice from behind them. It was the Phantom Virus. "The game ends now," he declared with a wild laugh.

Scooby and Cyber-Scooby's teeth were chattering.

"Like, we're about to become Scooby Snacks ourselves," said Shaggy.

"Maybe we can lose them in the amusement park!" suggested Fred. "Let's run for it!"

They took off, with the villains chasing after them. They were running so fast when they went through the gate into the amusement park that they flew off in opposite directions. The villains did the same.

The Tar Monster chased Shaggy and Cyber-Shaggy to the "Test Your Strength" game. They were able to get away when Cyber-Shaggy smashed the Tar Monster's foot with his mallet.

The Creeper followed Daphne and Cyber-Daphne into the haunted house. Fortunately, they found a trap door and tricked him into falling through it.

Fred and Cyber-Fred landed on the roller coaster — with the Gator Ghoul several cars behind them and gaining fast. They managed to jump off onto the Moon Bounce, leaving the Gator Ghoul on a wild ride.

Meanwhile, Old Iron Face chased Velma and

Cyber-Velma into the wax museum. They almost lost their glasses when they panicked and crashed into each other, but then they tripped Old Iron Face into a vat of hot wax.

Out on the merry-go-round, Scooby and Cyber-Scooby were being chased by Jaguaro. They got hold of the controls and made the merry-go-round spin so fast that Jaguaro flew off it!

"Great work, you guys!" said Cyber-Fred, coming up to the Scoobies.

They just stared at him and backed away, looking scared.

"What's the matter?" asked Fred.

Cyber-Scooby pointed behind Fred. A snarling Gator Ghoul was just about to pounce on him.

"I thought we lost him!" cried Cyber-Fred.

Just then, Shaggy and Cyber-Shaggy ran up to Fred. "The Tar Monster is right behind us, and boy is he mad!" they yelled.

"C'mon, everybody!" shouted Fred. "Let's get out of here!"

CHAPTER NINE

Everybody took off in different directions to fight it out with the villains from the gang's past.

Daphne and Cyber-Daphne met up with the Creeper in the Old Western Saloon. He burst through the swinging doors, looking for trouble — and the Daphnes gave it to him! They convinced him to have his picture taken dressed up like a cowboy. Cyber-Daphne handed him a holder full of flash powder. Daphne ducked behind the camera curtain.

There was a huge explosion! After the smoke cleared, the Creeper's face was all blackened with ash. He stared at Daphne and Cyber-Daphne, then fell over like a stiff board. Daphne and Cyber-Daphne left him lying there.

Meanwhile, in the amusement park, Velma and Cyber-Velma were wandering through the petting zoo. They were petting a baby goat when Old Iron Face snuck up behind them.

The baby goat's papa didn't seem to like Old Iron Face. He chased him off, butting him with his sharp horns. Velma and Cyber-Velma laughed as they watched Old Iron Face get butted by the papa goat.

Over at the bumper cars, Fred and Cyber-Fred were driving identical cars decorated like the Mystery Machine. Then the Gator Ghoul showed up, driving a car of his own.

Fred and Cyber-Fred drove toward the Gator Ghoul's car from opposite sides, shoving him toward the wall at top speed. The Gator Ghoul's bumper car hit the wall and he was launched into the air like a rocket! He flew over the railing and into a nearby dunk tank.

Fred and Cyber-Fred just smiled at each other and bumped their cars together for fun.

Where did Shaggy and Cyber-Shaggy end up? At the concession stand, naturally! Shaggy went over to the cotton candy machine. He stuck a cone inside, twirled it to fill it with cotton candy, and handed it to — the Tar Monster! Oops! Cyber-Shaggy and Shaggy each grabbed a soda gun from the soda fountain and fired away, blasting the Tar Monster until he fell into the cotton candy machine and got all wrapped up like a huge, pink mummy. Shaggy went over and grabbed a pinch to eat.

Then they ran to meet the rest of the gang. Everybody was there — except the Scoobies! "Scooby-Dooby-Doo! Where are you?" called Velma and Cyber-Velma.

The Scoobies were over at the log flume ride, enjoying a trip on the rushing water. Until Jaguaro, riding on his own log, bumped into them from behind. The Scoobies put their paws in the water and paddled as fast as they could to get away, but Jaguaro stuck with them.

Whoa! The Scoobies spotted a huge drop coming up. They jumped out of their log and right over

Jaguaro, then started doggie-paddling against the current. Jaguaro roared at them, but his log went over the edge and landed in the water below with a huge crash.

The Scoobies ran to join the gang.

"All right!" said Fred. "Now we just have one last villain to face. The Phantom Virus!"

"We need a plan," said the Velmas.

"Hey! Like, what's this?" Shaggy asked, pulling the long, flat, black magnet out of his pocket. "Zoinks! I forgot I still had this!"

Cyber-Shaggy stared at the magnet, going into a deep trance. Cyber-Velma was in a trance, too. So were Cyber-Scooby, Cyber-Daphne, and Cyber-Fred.

"Hmm! The cyber-gang is made of the same electromagnetic energy as the Phantom Virus," Fred said.

Shaggy put the magnet back in his pocket, and the cyber-gang snapped out of their trance.

"We got a way to beat the Phantom Virus," Fred told the cyber-gang. "Now we just have to track him down."

"I have a feeling we'll find him in there," Velma said, pointing to the video arcade. It was all lit up with blinking lights. The gang started walking into the arcade, and the cyber-gang followed.

Fred put out an arm to stop them. "We need you guys to stand guard out here," he said. He didn't want the cyber-gang to get hypnotized when the gang used the magnet against the Phantom Virus.

"Are you sure?" asked Cyber-Fred. He didn't even remember being in a trance.

"Trust us," said Velma. "It's best if you stay out here."

CHAPTER TEN

"Man, this is one great arcade," Shaggy said, when they got inside and saw dozens of video games, plus air hockey, Skee-Ball and basketball.

"Look!" said Daphne. There, at the far end of the arcade, was the Scooby-Doo video game. And sitting on top of it was a box of Scooby Snacks.

They had all started toward the Scooby video game when the maniacal laughter of the Virus echoed through the arcade. The gang froze and looked around. Suddenly, the Scooby video game exploded, revealing the Phantom Virus.

"Zoinks!" said Shaggy. It was the Phantom Virus. He laughed his wild laugh as every video game in the arcade came to life. Wild beams of electricity shot through the air. Basketballs, Skee-Balls and pinballs flew off the tables and toward the gang.

"Get your magnet, Shaggy!" Fred yelled.

Shaggy pulled out his magnet.

"Get closer to him!" shouted Velma.

Beams of electricity shot toward Shaggy, and he ducked. "Easy for you to say," he said.

"Toss it here!" Fred called.

"Like, with pleasure!" Shaggy threw the magnet to Fred.

Velma, Scooby, and Daphne ducked down to avoid the flying balls.

Fred moved toward the Phantom Virus, holding up the magnet. The Phantom Virus was still laughing, holding up his arms as if he were conducting the chaos in the arcade. Then Fred got closer, and the Phantom Virus suddenly started to break up.

All the games shut down. There were no more noises, no more beams of electricity, no more flying balls.

"You did it, Fred!" Velma cried. "Scooby, go grab the Scooby Snacks!"

"And hurry!" Fred said, still holding up the magnet. "I don't know how long this thing will work." He took a step forward, right onto a basketball. He fell hard. The magnet flew out of his hand and slid under a nearby video game, out of the gang's reach.

"Oh, no!" cried Daphne.

The Phantom Virus came to life again, and so did the arcade. Laughter, noise, electricity, and flying balls filled the air once more.

The virus shot a beam at a video game next to Fred. The game came to life. Wires shot out of it and wrapped around Fred's legs.

The gang split up and ducked behind different games.

The Phantom Virus just laughed. "If you thought my hitting was good, wait till you see my pitching!" he howled. With that, he waved his hand in the air and created a ball of energy. He wound up like a pitcher and threw the ball toward the game Shaggy was hiding behind. The ball slammed into the game.

"What do we do now?" Shaggy screamed.

Outside, the cyber-gang were worried at all the flashing lights and explosions emitting from the arcade.

Cyber-Daphne looked concerned. "Looks like they're in trouble!"

Cyber-Shaggy was very nervous. "Like, we've got to do something!"

Just then, they heard deep growls from behind them. The Tar Monster, the Creeper, the Gator Ghoul, Jaguaro, and Old Iron Face were charging toward them!

The cyber-gang screamed and ran in every direction.

In the confusion, Cyber-Scooby managed to slip away. He sneaked into the arcade.

Back inside, the Phantom Virus threw ball after ball at the gang.

Suddenly, Cyber-Scooby showed up, crawling low to the ground. He scampered over to Scooby and whispered into his ear. The Scoobies looked at each other and nodded. Then Cyber-Scooby stood up and began waving his paws and barking.

The Phantom Virus launched a ball at him. Cyber-Scooby ducked and the ball hit a foosball game behind him, destroying it.

Meanwhile, the real Scooby began creeping along the floor.

"You're down to your final out!" yelled the Phantom Virus, tossing another ball.

Cyber-Scooby jumped to avoid it. Real Scooby kept on creeping across the floor.

"I get it," said Fred. "Cyber-Scooby is distracting the Phantom Virus while Scooby gets the Snacks!"

"Scooby's almost there!" yelled Velma.

Sure enough, Scooby had reached the box of Scooby-Snacks. He grabbed it.

"He got them!" yelled Shaggy. "All right, Scooby!"

"No!" screamed the Virus. He looked horrified as he began to break up. All the flying objects fell onto the floor. The loud sounds and wild lights suddenly stopped.

Outside, the cyber-gang were cornered by the villains from the past. Just as they were about to lose hope, the villains all broke up electronically and disappeared.

Back inside, the Phantom Virus put his hands to his head, let out a bloodcurdling scream, and disintegrated and disappeared, right in front of the gang.

The arcade went quiet once more.

The cyber-gang ran in. "You did it," said Cyber-Fred. "You beat the Phantom Virus!"

"That's why he kept chasing us," Velma said. "He knew if we got the final box of Scooby Snacks, he would be destroyed."

Scooby walked over to Cyber-Scooby, still carrying the box of Scooby Snacks. The two Scoobies hugged. Then Scooby opened the box and gave a Scooby Snack to Cyber-Scooby.

CHAPTER ELEVEN

"I don't get it," said Daphne. "How come we're not being transported anywhere?"

"Like, we won the game," Shaggy told her. "There are no more levels." Scooby handed him a Scooby Snack, and Shaggy tossed it into the air, caught it in his mouth, and gulped it down.

"You mean, we're trapped here forever?" Daphne asked.

Cyber-Fred put a hand on her shoulder. "No," he said. "Your big reward is coming."

Just then, the entire arcade faded away. Suddenly everyone was standing outside. They looked up and saw a grid forming on the sky.

"Looks like we're leaving." Fred pointed up to the sky. The grid started to form a circular portal.

Everyone exchanged sad looks. "Sorry, but we have to go," said Velma.

Cyber-Velma gave a slow wave as the cyber-gang stepped away.

"Thanks for everything," Fred said.

"Like, be sure to look us up if you're ever in the cyber-world again," Cyber-Shaggy said.

Crack! A huge bolt of green light beamed out of the portal. The gang was engulfed by the beam and turned into grids. Then they were sucked up into the portal.

The next thing they knew, the gang was shot back out — right into Dr. Kaufman's lab! "You're back!" cried Eric. He and Dr. Kaufman were standing there, along with Bill and Officer Wembley.

"This is fascinating," said Dr. Kaufman, rubbing his hands together. "You must tell us what happened to you in cyberspace."

"Well, you don't have to worry about the Phantom Virus anymore," Fred told him.

"D-did you find out who created him?" Bill asked.

"We've got a pretty good idea," Fred answered.

"Excellent," said Dr. Kaufman, banging his fist down on the table. "Whoever created that virus will be severely punished."

Velma smiled at him. "At first we thought it was you, Dr. Kaufman," she said.

"What?" Dr. Kaufman stared at her. "But — but I'm a scientist! I've dedicated my life to this university!"

"We thought maybe you wanted to scare Eric and Bill off so you could enter that big International Science Fair contest using their work and collect the award money."

"Preposterous!" shouted Dr. Kaufman.

"Like, then there was another suspect," Shaggy said. "Grumpy old Officer Wembley."

"What?" Officer Wembley's face was redder than ever. "I've never committed a crime in my life!"

"But you were the only person in the lab with us when we got sent into the game," Daphne pointed out.

"Or so we thought," Fred added.

"But then once we got into the game," Velma said, "We found all these clues that pointed to the same person."

Daphne nodded. "Our first clue came when we were on the moon level. The Phantom Virus shouted 'Play ball!'"

"Then," Fred said, "In the Colosseum we found lines on the ground, shaped like a large diamond."

Now the gang was cooking.

"But our biggest clue came in the final level," Velma said.

Fred picked up the story. "The Phantom Virus was in the batting cage."

"And he said the final level was the major leagues," Daphne went on.

Eric scratched his head. "All I'm getting is that the Phantom Virus had a thing for baseball." He looked puzzled.

"Exactly!" Velma held up a finger. "And computer viruses usually reflect the personality of their creator!"

At that, everyone turned to look at Bill. He dashed for the door and jiggled the handle. "Of all the luck," he said. "It's locked."

"Not so fast, kid," said Officer Wembley.

Bill panicked and ran off to an area with rows of shelves. He tried another door but Scooby and the gang came and blocked his way.

Bill quickly turned and tried to head back but was blocked by Officer Wembley. As Bill backed up, Scooby used his tail to trip him. He stumbled as he fell, knocking a shelf down.

Officer Wembley quickly handcuffed the dazed student. "Okay son, it's all over."

"Bill!" said Eric. "You were my partner!"

"And you were my best student," added Dr. Kaufman.

"But I wasn't your favorite," Bill said.

"Huh?" Eric looked puzzled again.

"Dr. Kaufman chose your game design over mine. And I've been working on the hyper-laser forever, but as soon as you joined the team you got equal credit." Bill looked sulky.

"So," said Velma. "Since you didn't want to enter as a team, you invented the Phantom Virus, hoping to scare Eric away."

"That's right," Bill admitted. "But instead of getting scared, Eric called you guys."

"And when you saw us trying to track down the Virus, *you* got scared and, like, beamed us into cyberspace." Shaggy shook his head.

"I've got one more baseball term for you, Bill," said Dr. Kaufman. "You're out! Out of this lab and out of this university."

Bill looked mad. "That prize should have been all mine," he said. "And it would have been, too —"

"If it weren't for that dog and us meddling kids!" the gang chorused, as if they knew exactly what he was going to say.

Everybody cracked up. Everybody except Bill, that is.

CHAPTER TWELVE

Later that day, the gang met Eric at the malt shop to celebrate solving the case. Shaggy and Scooby sat at the counter eating cheeseburgers, and the rest of the gang sat at a table with Eric. He had his laptop computer with him.

"Dinner's on me, guys," Eric told them. "I want to thank you for your help. We'd never have gotten rid of that virus without you."

Shaggy swiveled around in his chair. "Like, you're paying? In that case, I'm having another cheeseburger."

Scooby swiveled around. "Two reeseburgers!" he said.

Velma and Daphne just shook their heads. "What's going to happen to Bill?" Velma asked Eric.

"Dr. Kaufman is already taking steps to have him expelled," Eric told her.

"What about the hyper-laser?" Fred asked.

Eric smiled. "Dr. Kaufman and I still plan to display it at the International Science Fair next month."

"That's wonderful, Eric," Daphne said.

"I just wish you guys didn't have to get trapped in cyberspace to solve this case," Eric told the gang.

Fred shrugged. "You know, it wasn't all that bad."

"Really?" Eric asked.

Velma nodded. "Going back in time was really cool. You did a great job designing all the levels."

"Thanks, Velma." Eric blushed.

"But, like, next time, go easier on the monsters," Shaggy said.

The rest of the gang laughed. Then Eric opened up his laptop and typed on a few keys. "Hey Shaggy," he said. "I just pulled up the Scooby-Doo game on my laptop. Want to play?"

Shaggy and Scooby swiveled around again. "What do you say, Scooby?" Shaggy asked. "Now there's no creepy Phantom Virus in the game."

Scooby nodded eagerly.

Velma looked doubtful. "Haven't you two had enough excitement for one day?" she asked.

Shaggy grinned at her. "What's playing a few games going to hurt?" he asked. He came over to the table and sat down next to Eric. Eric turned the laptop toward him. Shaggy started to punch the keys. "Zoinks!" he said suddenly.

Daphne gasped. "Is it the Phantom Virus?" she asked.

"No," Shaggy said. "Look."

Everyone gathered around the screen.

There on the screen, the entire cyber-gang was smiling and waving back at the gang in the malt shop.

The gang waved back.

Scooby reached a paw over and slid the laptop away from Shaggy.

"Hey! What are you doing, Scooby?" Shaggy asked.

Scooby started typing. On the screen, a box of Scooby Snacks suddenly appeared right next to Cyber-Scooby. Cyber-Scooby's smile grew larger when he saw them.

"Now that's what I call hacking," said Daphne.

"Like, hacking — and Scooby snacking!" Shaggy added.

The whole gang cracked up.

Scooby raised his paws into the air in triumph. "Scooby-Dooby-Doo!"